Hide AND Seek with Grandpa

Rob Lewis

RED FOX

D0994767

A Red Fox Book

Published by Random House Children's Books
20 Vauxhall Bridge Road, London SW1V 2SA

A division of Random House UK Ltd
London Melbourne Sydney Auckland
Johannesburg and agencies throughout the world

3 5 7 9 10 8 6 4 2

First published in Great Britain by Red Fox 1997

Printed in Hong Kong

RANDOM HOUSE UK Limited Reg. No. 954009

ISBN 0 09 971221 0

SPECIAL
SUNDAYS

'Does Grandpa get lonely?' asked Finley.

'I don't think so,' said Mum.

'But he lives all on his own,' said Finley.

'I'm sure he keeps busy,' said Mum.

Finley thought about Grandpa all on
his own.

'I will visit him after school,' he said.

'Ben is coming to play after school,'
said Mum.

'He can come another day,' said Finley.

After school Finley went to Grandpa's
house. But Grandpa was just leaving.
'Sorry, Finley,' said Grandpa. 'I'm going
fossil hunting with Fred from next door.'
'Oh,' said Finley.

Finley went home again. He telephoned

Ben. But Ben had gone out.

Finley sat all on his own.

'I will visit Grandpa tomorrow,' he said.

'You are going skating with Sally and Joe tomorrow,' Mum said.

'I can go with Ben on Friday,' said Finley.

After school Finley went to Grandpa's
house again. Grandpa was putting on
his coat.

'Sorry Finley,' he said. 'It's weight training
night. I won't be back until late.'
'Really,' said Finley.

Finley went home. Sally and Joe had already gone skating. He sat all on his own.

'I will try again tomorrow,' he sighed.

'You are going swimming with the Smithsons tomorrow,' Mum said.

'I can go swimming next week,' said Finley.

After school Finley ran to Grandpa's house. There were a lot of people outside.

'Sorry, Finley,' said Grandpa. 'We are all going hang-gliding this evening.'
'You're kidding,' said Finley.

Finley went home. He sat all on his own.

'Grandpa is very busy,' said Mum.

'Grandpa is too busy!' said Finley, crossly.

The next day Grandpa had tea with Fred.

'Finley has called three times this week,'
Grandpa said.

'Perhaps he is lonely,' said Fred.

'I will visit him tonight,' decided Grandpa.

'You have brick-laying class tonight,'
said Fred.

'I can miss one week,' said Grandpa.

After school Grandpa went round to
Finley's house.

'Sorry,' said Mum. 'Finley has gone skating
with Ben.'

Grandpa went home. He sat all on his own.

After skating, Finley telephoned Grandpa.

'We are both very busy,' said Finley. 'We

must choose a day when we are *not* busy.'

'We could meet on Sundays,' said Grandpa.

'OK,' said Finley. 'We will keep

Sundays special.'

HIDE AND
SEEK

One Sunday, Grandpa and Finley were playing Hide and Seek.

'I will hide first,' said Finley.

'OK,' said Grandpa. 'I will count to twenty.'

'Count slowly,' said Finley.

Grandpa counted to twenty, slowly.

Then he went to look for Finley.

Grandpa looked among the cabbages.

Then he looked in the garage.

Finley hid in the blackcurrant bushes.

He waited a long time.

Grandpa was not very good at Hide and

Seek. Finley went to look for him.

Grandpa was leaning over the fence. He was talking to Fred.

'Sorry, Finley,' said Grandpa. 'Fred was just showing me one of his fossils.'

'I will hide again,' said Finley.

'OK,' said Grandpa.

Grandpa counted to twenty.

Finley hid in the greenhouse.

Grandpa looked behind the garden canes
and under the wheelbarrow.

Then he wandered round to the front
garden...

Finley waited in the greenhouse. He waited a long time...

He went to look for Grandpa in the rhubarb.

Then he went round to the front garden. Grandpa was weeding.

'Um, sorry, Finley,' said Grandpa. 'I noticed a few weeds that needed pulling up.'

'I will hide again,' sighed Finley.

'I will count to twenty again,' said Grandpa.

'Just count to ten,' said Finley.

Grandpa counted to ten.

First he searched the compost heap.

Then he looked behind the deck chair...

Finley hid in the water barrel. He hid for a long time. Then he heard a noise. Someone was snoring. Grandpa had fallen asleep in the deck chair.

'Wake up, Grandpa,' shouted Finley.
'Sorry,' said Grandpa, yawning. 'I was thinking about where you were hiding.'
'I'm sure,' said Finley. 'Let's play somewhere else.'

'OK,' said Grandpa. 'I know a good place.'
Grandpa led Finley to the bottom of the
garden. He opened the gate that led into
the wood.

'This is a better place,' he said. 'I will hide this time.'

'Don't fall asleep,' said Finley.

'Just start counting,' said Grandpa.

'Grandpa is not very good at Hide and Seek,' said Finley to himself. 'I will count to thirty this time.'

Finley counted to thirty. Then he went to look for Grandpa.

There were a lot of big trees to hide
behind. Grandpa was not behind any of
them. Finley went deeper into the wood.

He looked under bushes. He searched piles
of leaves. He peered under logs. There was
no sign of Grandpa.

'Grandpa has got lost!' he grumbled. Finley followed the path back to the house. But the path did not go back to the house. 'Now I'm lost,' said Finley, worriedly.

'Found you!' said a voice. Finley looked up.

Grandpa was sitting in a tree. 'I thought

you were doing the finding,' he said.

WORMS

'Finley,' called Mum. 'Will you take something round to Grandpa's house for me?'

'OK, Mum,' said Finley.

'It's on the table in the hall,' called Mum.

'Fine,' said Finley.

'Don't let them escape,' said Mum.

'No, Mum,' said Finley.

But Finley wasn't listening. He was busy watching the television.

After the programme had finished it was time to go to Grandpa's house. Finley picked up the plastic bag.

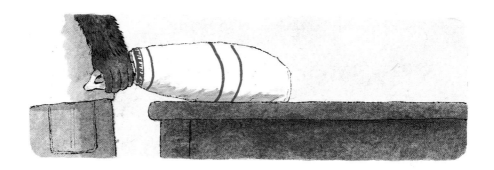

He walked to the bus stop. He waited in the queue.

A lady gave him a funny look. Something was tickling her leg.

'Stop tickling my leg,' she said crossly.

'I'm not,' said Finley.

Finley got on the bus.

A big lady sat down beside him. There was not much room for Finley. He looked out of the window.

'Eeeeeek!' shrieked the lady. 'There's a worm on my lap.'

Finley looked in Grandpa's bag.

It was full of worms.

'Sorry,' he said.

The worms kept escaping from the bag. They were crawling all over the floor. Soon everybody was shrieking. Finley had to get off the bus.

He decided to walk to Grandpa's house.

On the way he bought some sweets.

He sat down on a bench to eat them.

There was a baby in a pushchair next to
the bench.

'Hello,' said Finley.

'Goo,' said the baby.

Finley looked for a bin for his sweet wrappers.

The baby looked at Grandpa's plastic bag.

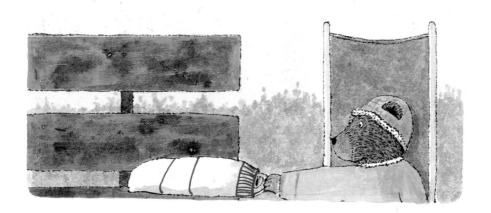

Finley put the wrappers in the bin.

The baby put his hand in Grandpa's bag.

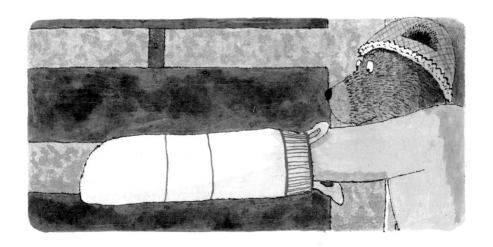

Finley ate his last sweet.

The baby ate a worm.

'Oh no!' cried Finley.

'Goo!' said the baby. Finley felt sick.

Finley hurried to Grandpa's house.
Birds flew round his head. They wanted
the worms in Grandpa's bag.

'Go away, birds!' shouted Finley.

At last Finley got to Grandpa's house.

'Here are your worms,' said Finley.

'I will catch some big fish with these,' said
Grandpa. 'Thank you.'

'No problem,' said Finley.

'Could you bring something else next
week?' said Grandpa.

'Not more worms,' said Finley, worriedly.

'Not worms,' said Grandpa. 'Maggots.'

'Oh no!' groaned Finley.